6
2/16
9/20

W9-ATR-141

The Painting That Wasn't There

by
Steve Brezenoff

★

illustrated by
C.B. Canga

STONE ARCH BOOKS
www.stonearchbooks.com

Field Trip Mysteries are published by Stone Arch Books
A Capstone Imprint
151 Good Counsel Drive, P.O. Box 669
Mankato, Minnesota 56002
www.capstonepub.com

Library of Congress Cataloging-in-Publication Data
Brezenoff, Steven.
   The painting that wasn't there / by Steve Brezenoff ;
illustrated by C.B. Canga.
      p. cm. — (Field trip mysteries)
   ISBN 978-1-4342-1608-3
[1. School field trips—Fiction. 2. Mystery and detective
stories.] I. Canga, C. B., ill. II. Title. III. Title:
Painting that was not there.
   PZ7.B7576Pai 2010
   [Fic]—dc22
      2009002572

Printed in the United States of America in Stevens Point, Wisconsin.
032010   005737R

Creative Director:
   Heather Kindseth
Graphic Designer:
   Carla Zetina-Yglesias

Dear pa

The si

We v
We'
fro

D

PRINTED IN
THE U.S.A.

Summary:
James "Gum" Shoo's art class heads to
the museum. They've been learning about
forged art, but they never expected to
find a fake in the gallery! Only Gum and
his gumshoe friends will be able to solve
this museum caper.

★ TABLE OF CONTENTS ★

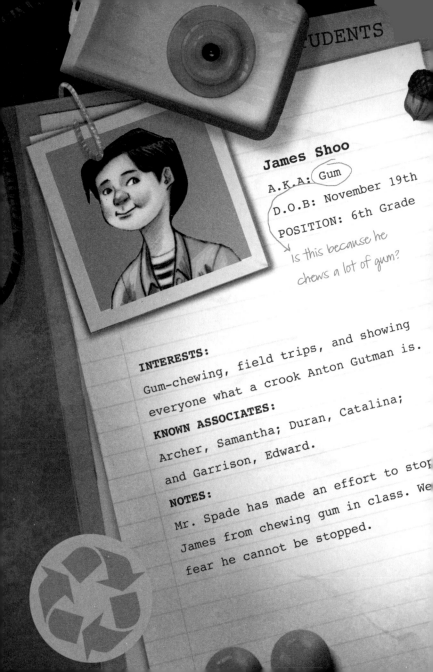

James Shoo

A.K.A: Gum

D.O.B: November 19th

POSITION: 6th Grade

Is this because he chews a lot of gum?

INTERESTS:

Gum-chewing, field trips, and showing everyone what a crook Anton Gutman is.

KNOWN ASSOCIATES:

Archer, Samantha; Duran, Catalina; and Garrison, Edward.

NOTES:

Mr. Spade has made an effort to stop James from chewing gum in class. We fear he cannot be stopped.

CHAPTER
ONE

GUM SHOO

My name is
James Shoo.
No one calls me that, though.
Everyone calls me
Gum instead.

Kids who don't know me too well think that's because I always chew gum, but they're wrong.

I mean, I do always chew gum. Gum is probably my favorite thing in the world. I love almost every flavor I've ever tried: watermelon, green apple, cotton candy . . . you name it. So I do chew gum pretty much nonstop when I'm awake.

My mom makes me eat other foods too, of course. It's hard to eat food of any kind while chewing gum. But once I finish eating, it's right back to the gum.

Still, that's not why I'm called Gum. Anton Gutman, this total dork in our class, says it's because "gum" rhymes with "dumb." That's one of many reasons my friends and I don't like Anton Gutman.

My best friends know the real reason I'm called Gum. Actually, my friend Sam — Samantha Archer, that is — gave me the name.

Sam lives with her grandparents, and she watches old detective movies with them all the time. So she's always using funny words and phrases normal people haven't said in like a hundred years. "Gumshoe" is one of those words, I guess.

Anyway, she started calling me Gum Shoo after our first adventure. That's what this story is about.

It all started in Ms. Stanwyck's art class.

MY FRIENDS

Every Monday afternoon, my sixth-grade class has art class. We get to leave our normal classroom and go down to the art room.

I love Monday afternoons. Pretty much everyone does. It's fun to leave Mr. Spade's class and go to Ms. Stanwyck's art class.

Her classroom is colorfully decorated, with paintings and photographs. It's different from our normal classroom.

I like Ms. Stanwyck because she never gives me a hard time about chewing gum in class.

My friend Egg loves art class more than most of us. He's really into photography, and some weeks, we take pictures.

"I really hope that Ms. Stanwyck is going to have us do photography today," Egg whispered to me as we headed down the hall.

Egg wasn't named for his favorite breakfast. His real name is Edward G. Garrison: E.G.G. So everyone just calls him Egg. Besides loving photography, he's also pretty much the shortest kid in our grade.

We were following single-file behind Mr. Spade, our teacher. Egg was walking right behind me. In front of me was our friend Cat, and in front of Cat was Sam.

Sam is the tallest kid in our grade. She's taller than Mr. Spade, even.

"You always say that!" Sam said to Egg. "We can't do photography in art class every week!"

Egg shrugged. "I don't see why not," he said. He raised his camera and snapped a photo of Sam.

That camera was always around Egg's neck. It's digital, but it's huge. It looks funny on such a little guy. It's almost bigger than he is.

"It doesn't matter anyway," Cat said. "Don't you remember? We're looking at paintings today."

"Oh, that's right," I said.

Right before we reached Ms. Stanwyck's class, I reached into my pocket and pulled out a fresh piece of gum. Orange-flavored gum, to be exact. The one in my mouth was losing its flavor: root beer float.

"Ms. Stanwyck told us last week that we'd be looking at paintings," Cat reminded us. "Sorry, Egg, no photography today."

"Oh well," Egg said. "Maybe next time. I guess paintings could be cool too."

We didn't realize it then, but our adventure was about to begin.

ART CLASS

When everybody reached the art class and sat down, Ms. Stanwyck gave us all a big smile.

She's a very nice lady. She's about as old as the hills, and she's even shorter than Egg. She always has a pair of old glasses hanging around her neck.

"Let's start by looking at a couple of paintings," our teacher said. Ms. Stanwyck switched off the lights and switched on the projector.

"Each of these paintings is considered a masterpiece," she said. "They have something else in common, though."

The first painting was of a man and his dog. The man was carrying a basket under one arm. The painting looked very old.

"This one is called 'After the Hunt,'" Ms. Stanwyck said. "It's by Jan Weenix. He painted it in 1665."

"Aw, cute, a doggy!" Cat called out. Some kids laughed. Cat sat back and smiled. She loves animals.

"Wait, what's in the basket?" Sam added, leaning forward.

"Whoa, it's a bunch of dead birds," I pointed out.

Cat's jaw dropped. "And is he also carrying a dead bunny?" she asked.

"That's right," Ms. Stanwyck replied. "Remember, it's called 'After the Hunt.'"

"I don't like it," Cat whispered.

Ms. Stanwyck clicked her controller and the next slide came up. This one looked like the inside of a barn. There were some people and horses.

"Ooh, horses!" Cat exclaimed.

"This painting is my favorite," Ms. Stanwyck said. "It is by a man named George Morland."

I looked at the painting.

"It's called 'The Inside of a Stable,' from 1791," Ms. Stanwyck went on. "It's considered Morland's finest work. Many young artists have made copies of it as they learned how to paint."

Ms. Stanwyck stopped and looked around the class. "Have any of you figured out what all of these paintings have in common?" she asked us.

Sam raised her hand. "Is it that they all have animals in them?" she asked.

Ms. Stanwyck nodded. "That's right, Samantha," she said. "Even more exciting, though, is that all the paintings I'm showing you today are on tour."

"On tour?" I said, laughing. "Like a band? I can't really see these paintings selling out the arena!"

"Well, something like that," Ms. Stanwyck said, smiling. "Sometimes very famous paintings are sent from city to city so people all over the world can see them in person."

"All these paintings are coming to River City?" Cat asked. She sounded excited. "A tour of animal paintings! I can't wait!"

"You won't have to wait long," Ms. Stanwyck said. "We'll be going on a field trip to the Art Museum next Monday."

"Yes!" I said, pumping my fist. "I love a good field trip."

"I'm glad you're all so excited," Ms. Stanwyck said. "I'm excited myself. The 'Inside of a Stable' is the featured painting. I haven't seen it since I made my own copy of it back in art school."

I frowned. This didn't make any sense to me at all. Why would she make a copy of a painting? "Ms. Stanwyck, I don't get it," I said.

"Why did you make a copy of a famous painting?" I asked.

"Can't you just scan it, or take a picture or something? Seems like a big pain to copy it!" I added.

Ms. Stanwyck smiled at me. "Well, James," she said, "we don't make copies just to have a copy. Young artists make copies to learn techniques, or to challenge themselves."

"Why do so many people copy this painting?" Cat said. "Is it because they think the small horse is cute?"

Ms. Stanwyck looked lovingly at the slide. Then she looked back at us.

"Not exactly. You see, students, George Morland's style is very casual," she said. "He never put a lot of work into his paintings. They were quickly done, and sometimes sloppy."

"So they're easier to copy?" asked Sam.

"Well, you'd think so . . . at first," Ms.
Stanwyck said. She smiled again.

"Many art students try to copy Morland's
strokes exactly," she told us. "That's very
difficult to do. If you look closely, you can
see where Morland did a stroke quickly."

Ms. Stanwyck pointed to the small
wheelbarrow in the corner of the painting.
"This part was difficult for me," she said.
"But you can see what a quick job Morland
made of it. It's very sloppy!"

She added, "Come and have a closer
look if you like. Then we'll move on to
some more paintings."

Sam, Egg, Cat, and I gathered around
the painting. Some other kids in the class
got up to look closer too.

Egg took a quick photo of the wheelbarrow. "You can see how the brush left a mark here," he said, pointing. "Cool!"

We had a look and then went to sit down. Ms. Stanwyck went on to show us about a million more paintings, but the real excitement started a week later.

THE MUSEUM

The next Monday, instead of going to Ms. Stanwyck's classroom for art, we all boarded a school bus for our field trip. Egg and I shared the last seat of the bus, and Sam and Cat sat across the aisle from us.

The road from the school to the Art Museum was very bumpy. Every bump we hit sent the four of us flying straight up. Sam almost banged her head on the bus ceiling like ten times. It was fun.

We hit another bump and Egg went flying. "Woo!" he cried out. He was the smallest, so he always got the most air. The camera around his neck almost fell off.

"Are you going to take photos of the paintings, Egg?" Cat asked. "And can I have copies?"

"Sure," Egg replied.

Ms. Stanwyck called back to us, "Remember, Edward: you can take photos, but don't use the flash."

Egg nodded. "I know," he said. "Because the flash can damage the paintings."

"That's right," Ms. Stanwyck said. "It can fade the colors."

Soon the bus pulled up to the curb in front of the museum. We all piled out onto the sidewalk. It was a very sunny morning.

We all gathered around Ms. Stanwyck and rushed into the museum. The entrance was amazing! It was this huge room, with a big dome ceiling. It looked like everything was made of marble and gold.

A few men and women in blue suits stood around. They all had badges on their jackets. One of them looked at us and said, "Shhh!"

"Sure is a lot of muscle in here," Sam muttered to us, frowning at the security guards.

Cat and Egg looked at me. "Huh?" they both said.

I whispered to my friends, "Sam means there are a lot of security guards. I think." Sometimes we need to help each other understand when Sam uses expressions from those old movies she loves.

Cat nodded. "Got it," she whispered back. Then the four of us followed the rest of the class.

Ms. Stanwyck led us down a long hallway. The walls were lined with loads of paintings, but none of them had any animals in them.

"Ms. Stanwyck," Cat called out, "wait just a second. There are no animals in these paintings!"

Ms. Stanwyck laughed. "Don't worry, Catalina," she said. "The exhibit we're here to see has a room all to itself, at the end of this hall."

Soon we came to an archway. We went through it into a huge circular room. I gasped. The room looked bigger than a football field!

The walls were covered with paintings. A circle of metal posts and a velvet rope made it impossible to get very close to the paintings.

"Wow," Egg whispered. Even though he was trying to be quiet, his voice bounced off the walls.

We walked lightly after Ms. Stanwyck, and our steps echoed and squeaked on the stone floor.

Ms. Stanwyck stopped right in the middle of the room. We all gathered around her.

"Okay, students," she said. "I want you to walk around and look at the paintings, and talk to each other about the paintings. In class next week, we'll discuss what we've seen here."

She looked at her watch. "The time is now eight o'clock. We will have three hours in the museum. Meet back here at eleven. No excuses for being late!"

"Yes, Ms. Stanwyck," the whole class said together.

Our group of four stuck together, as usual. That's what best friends do, even on field trips.

"Look at this one," Cat cried out. She grabbed Sam and pulled her toward a painting. Egg and I followed them.

Cat had taken us to a painting of two horses, one black and one white.

A man in blue was sitting on the black one. Both horses were having a drink from a small pond.

"I like the white horse," Cat said. "This is an awesome painting."

Sam shrugged. "It's okay, I guess," she said. "It's nothing special, though. Just a couple of old horses."

Egg scratched his chin. "I wonder why that guy has two horses," he said. His glasses slid down his nose and he pushed them back up.

I leaned on Egg's shoulder. "Who knows!" I said. "Maybe he was out riding the black horse and this white horse just started following him."

"Right," Sam said, laughing. "So the guy in blue thinks, 'Hey, free horse! I'm going to keep him.'"

"That's probably what I'd think," I replied.

"Me too," Egg said. "I like it. I think I'm going to take pictures of all of our favorites."

We all made room so that he could take a good photo. Then Egg snapped a few pictures of other paintings, too.

"Hey!" someone shouted.

The four of us spun around.

It was the security guard who had shushed us earlier.

"No flash photography!"

he said.

The security guard walked over to us and grabbed Egg's collar and his camera.

Egg cowered. "The flash didn't go off," he said, stuttering a little. Egg gets nervous sometimes. "I know that's bad for the paintings. I wouldn't use a flash around them. I swear."

Egg was right, I'm sure of it. There was no flash when he took the picture.

So I said so. "He's right, mister. The flash didn't go off."

Sam and Cat nodded. "He knows a lot about photography," Cat added.

The guard glared at us. "This is your first and only warning," he said. Then he handed Egg his camera, let go of his collar, and walked off.

THE SUSPECTS

The four of us huddled together. "What was that all about?" Cat asked in a whisper.

Sam squinted at the security guard, whose back was to us. "I don't know," she said. "But he's cruising for a bruising."

Sam was talking like an old-time detective again.

"Is he?" Egg asked.

Sam nodded. "Yep," she said. "If he keeps giving you a hard time, Egg, he's in trouble with me."

Suddenly, Cat clapped her hands together. "Look!" she said. "It's the painting Ms. Stanwyck loved so much."

We all turned and looked where Cat was looking.

She was right. It was the painting Ms. Stanwyck had copied in school: "The Inside of a Stable," by George Morland.

Most of our classmates were already surrounding the painting. Of course, no one could get too close, because of the velvet rope.

Even the security guard had gone over there. I guess that was because the crowd was so big.

The group of us had made him pretty nervous, too. He was all shaky and sweating. Most days he doesn't usually have to watch so many people at once!

We walked over to the group.

"I can't get very close," Cat said, sadly.

"Wait a few minutes," I replied. "People will move on to other paintings pretty soon."

"I don't need to wait," Egg said. "I can sneak through the crowd and snap a quick shot."

He started to weave through the group of students.

"Watch yourself, Egg," Sam called after him. "That goon has his eye on you."

Egg turned around and looked at me.

"She means the security guard," I said. "No flash photos."

Egg nodded. "I know," he said. "Don't worry." With that, he slid into the crowd and vanished.

A moment later, though, the security guard screamed, "Hey! I said no flash photography!"

He dove into the crowd of students. Soon he had Egg by the collar in one hand, and Egg's camera in the other hand.

"My flash didn't go off," Egg shouted in reply.

The guard put Egg down at the back of the crowd, next to Ms. Stanwyck.

"I promise, Ms. Stanwyck," Egg pleaded. "My flash didn't go off!"

"I'm sorry," the guard said, "but I'm going to have to confiscate this camera until your group leaves the museum at eleven."

"No way," Egg said. "I need my camera. I have to have my camera. That is totally unfair. Please, I swear, I didn't use a flash, and I need to have my camera!"

Ms. Stanwyck looked at the guard, then at Egg. "Edward," she said, "the guard has to have the final say in this matter."

"But, Ms. Stanwyck . . . ," Egg started to say, but Ms. Stanwyck stopped him by putting up her hand.

"Now, Edward," she said, frowning at him, "it's really not like you to talk back. You will have your camera back in a few hours."

"Yes, Ms. Stanwyck," Egg said, looking at his feet.

"Good," Ms. Stanwyck said. "Now go enjoy the museum with your friends."

Egg walked over to me, Sam, and Cat. "I can't believe this!" he shouted. "This is so unfair."

Sam put a hand on his shoulder. "It's okay, Egg," she said. "That stooge had it in for you, but you'll get your camera back."

"Oh, I know that," Egg said. "But there's something else."

Cat, Sam, and I glanced at each other. "What else?" I asked finally.

"The painting by Morland," Egg said. "I got a good look at it with my telephoto lens."

"And?" Cat prompted.

Egg took a deep breath and pushed his glasses up his nose. "It's a copy," he said. "A fake!"

BATHROOM BUST

"A fake?" I said, shocked. "How can you tell?"

"Yeah, Egg," Sam added. "How do you know the picture's a phony?"

"I got a very good look at the bottom right corner," Egg said. "I wanted to see the wheelbarrow Ms. Stanwyck talked about."

"The part she said was hard to copy?" Cat asked.

Egg nodded. "Right," he said. "Well, in the painting up there, you can tell it's not his sloppy quick strokes. You can tell the person who painted that painting was being really, really careful."

"Like someone was trying too hard?" Sam asked.

Egg nodded again. "Exactly," he said. "Not like someone was being fast. Like they were being slow and taking their time."

"Why would the museum hang up a fake painting?" I asked.

Not that I didn't trust Egg. It was just that it didn't make sense. Why would a museum have a fake in its collection? I didn't get it.

"I get it," Sam said.

"You do?" I asked, feeling confused.

Sam nodded slowly. "I can see it now," she said.

"Well, you're going to have to explain it to me," I told her. "Because I don't get it and I can't see it."

Sam smiled. "With all this muscle around, these paintings must be worth a pretty penny," she began.

"Obviously," I said. "They hired a lot of security to protect the paintings."

"Right," Sam said. She thought for a second. "So if someone made a copy of one of the paintings," she went on, "that person could switch it with the real painting on the wall. Then the crook would have the real painting, which is worth a fortune! Maybe millions!"

"Whoa," Egg said. "Millions?"

Sam shrugged.

"Could be. I've heard of paintings selling for hundreds of millions of dollars."

"Then if that's a copy of the Morland horse painting," Cat said, "shouldn't we tell Ms. Stanwyck?"

"Or the police?" I added.

Sam shook her head. "No proof," she said.

"Right," Egg added, nodding. "The security guard took my camera. The photo I took of the wheelbarrow is still in it."

"So?" I said. "The painting itself is right there on the wall. Anyone can just walk up to it and check it out!"

"Not really," Cat said. "The velvet rope makes it impossible to get close."

We all fell silent and thought about it.

Sam finally spoke. "You know what we have to do," she said. "Solve this crime ourselves."

She and I looked at each other and nodded. "Okay," I said.

Egg nodded and said, "I'm in. Definitely."

Cat sighed. "You guys," she said. "Fine. Me too."

Sam beamed. "All right," she said. "A real mystery. First, we need a list of suspects!"

"Anton Gutman," I said right away. "He's the suspect at the top of the list."

"Anton?" Cat asked. "What does he have to do with it?"

I shrugged. "Whatever," I said. "I don't like him!"

"Fine," Sam said. "So Anton is on our suspect list. But who else?"

"Isn't it obvious?" Cat whispered. "It was Ms. Stanwyck!"

I nearly fell over. "Ms. Stanwyck?" I said. "Are you crazy? Why would she steal the painting?"

Sam stroked her chin. "Maybe Cat has a point," she said. "We already know she made a copy of the painting in question. She admitted that much in class last week, remember?"

"That's true," I said, nodding.

"Plus," Sam put in, "she knows everything about Morland and this painting. Even from ten feet away, she must have been able to spot a fake. Why didn't she say anything?"

"Hm," Egg added. "She did let that security guard take my camera, too."

"The only evidence," Sam pointed out.

"Okay then," I said firmly. "Fine. I'll add Ms. Stanwyck to the suspect list."

Just then, the security guard came over.

"What are you kids up to over here?" the guard asked.

"Nothing, sir," Cat replied with a big smile.

The guard eyed Egg. "Make sure it stays that way," the guard said. He glared at each of us, then walked off.

As the security guard walked away, a weird guy in a long coat knocked into him.

"Excuse me," the weird guy said.

Something fell out of the guard's back pocket.

"What's that?" I said, pointing.

Cat jogged over and scooped it up. "Sir!" she started to call out. But then she suddenly stopped.

Cat came darting back over to us.

"Guys," she said. "Check this out." She held out a folded piece of thick paper.

"A brochure?" Egg said.

Sam grabbed it and looked at the cover. "Not just any brochure," she said. "It's a brochure for an art school!"

"The guard is an art student too?" I said.

"Plus he has access to the museum and all the paintings," Cat added.

"You know what that means," Egg said.

Sam nodded and whispered, "It means our suspect list just got one name longer."

AHA!

"So," I said, popping a fresh piece of strawberry-banana gum into my mouth, "our suspects so far are Ms. Stanwyck, the security guard who took Egg's camera, and . . ."

Just then, someone bumped into me.

Anton Gutman.

"Oh, sorry," Anton said, laughing.

He and two of his weaselly friends were walking past us, giggling and hiding something.

"What are those clowns up to?" Sam asked.

I shrugged. "No good, I bet," I said.

We watched as Anton and his friends went into the nearest restroom.

"Let's follow them," Sam said.

"Gross!" Cat replied quickly.

Sam rolled her eyes. "We have to see what they're hiding," she said.

"We'll go," I said, taking Egg by the arm.

"Wait a second. What? We will?" Egg protested. But I pulled him along next to me.

Quietly, I pushed the bathroom door open. Anton and his friends were standing, thick as thieves, at the sinks. They were still giggling.

They didn't hear us come in.

"Aha!" I shouted, pointing at them. "Caught you!"

The three hoodlums jumped.

But they weren't huddling around any stolen painting. Instead, they were busy writing their names on the bathroom mirror.

"What do you think you're doing?" I said when I saw the permanent markers in their hands.

They glanced over at me and Egg. I guess they figured we couldn't stop them.

Anton just laughed and turned back to the mirror.

"Go away, losers," he said.

I was ready to get out of there. Anton wasn't the crook.

I thought Egg was turning to leave. But instead, he turned and opened the bathroom door. Then he shouted out into the hallway, "Guard!"

"Hey!" Anton yelled. "Shut up, Egg!"

But it was too late. The security guard came running. Egg and I got out of the way and watched the guard drag away Anton's gang by the collars.

Egg and I walked back over to Cat and Sam and told them what had happened. "Well, I guess Anton isn't a suspect anymore," I said.

"Yeah," Egg agreed. "He's still a jerk, though."

"I can't believe you called the guard," Cat said.

Egg laughed. "Me either. But those guys deserve it."

"Totally," Cat said. "I mean, are we in third grade anymore? Who writes their name in the bathroom? How stupid."

"Back to the mystery, guys. So if Anton isn't a suspect, that leaves Ms. Stanwyck and the guard," Sam said, counting on her fingers.

Just then, I spotted that weird guy in the long coat again. This time he was skulking around near the Morland painting.

I elbowed Sam.

"Look at that guy.
Doesn't he look
shady?"
I said.

Sam nodded slowly. "Definitely," she replied. "Why is he hanging around by the Morland painting?"

"Pretty suspicious," Egg agreed.

The four of us moved in to check out the weird guy. "Here," Sam said. We followed her into a doorway near the Morland painting and huddled together.

"He's hiding something under that coat, I bet," Sam said.

"Yeah," Cat agreed. "It's too hot out for a coat like that."

"Exactly," Sam said. "In the old movies crooks wears coats like that all the time. He's involved with this crime, I'd bet."

"I'm with Sam," I said, nodding. "He looks like a crook."

Suddenly, a voice came from behind us. "All right, Mel," the voice said. "My shift is over. I'll see you tomorrow."

It was the security guard who took Egg's camera. The doorway we had hidden in was the entrance to the security guards' break room.

We turned to look. The guard was picking up a long black case.

"What have you got there, Tom?" the other guard said. That must have been Mel. Tom was the guard who had taken Egg's camera, of course.

Tom looked at the case in his hand. "What, this?" he said. "Oh, it's just my pool cue."

"Off to shoot some pool this afternoon?" Mel asked.

"That's right," Tom replied. "Well, I'll see ya tomorrow."

With that, the guard started walking toward us. He stopped when he reached the doorway.

"You kids sneaking around again?" he asked. "Don't worry. Mel in there will give your camera back when your group is ready to leave."

The man shook his head and started walking off.

"Speaking of that," I said, "what time is it, Egg?"

Egg looked at his wrist. "It's ten thirty," he replied.

"Ten thirty?!" Sam said. "That only gives us thirty minutes to crack this case!"

CASE CRACKED!

"Okay," I said. "Let's think."

Cat nodded and said, "Right. What do we know?"

Sam took a deep breath. "We know that Ms. Stanwyck knows everything about Morland," she said. "And we know she made a copy of 'The Inside of a Stable.'"

"We know the guard is in art school," Egg added, "or thinking about going to art school."

"Right," Cat said. "So he may have made a copy of the Morland painting too."

"And," Sam added, "we spotted that shady guy skulking near the painting."

I shook my head. "This is getting us nowhere," I said. "We must be missing something."

The four of us leaned against the cold marble wall. I was feeling pretty down about this mystery.

From where I was standing, I could see a cleaning crew.

A couple of men in green uniforms were taking down a painting. First they pulled the painting off the wall. Then one man pulled the frame off.

Without the frame, the painting was just a big piece of canvas.

The second man picked up the canvas and rolled it up, like a poster. Then he slid it into a long case with a zipper at the top.

"That's it!" I shouted, jumping to my feet.

"What's it?" Sam said.

"No time to explain," I replied. "Just follow me. We have to run!"

I started down the hall toward the main entrance. My sneakers squeaked on the hard floor. The sound echoed through the museum. My three best friends were close at my heels.

"Where are we going?" Sam said as she caught up to me. Sam is very fast.

"We have to catch that security guard before he leaves," I replied between breaths.

I looked around. The guard was slowly walking toward the exit. "See you tomorrow, guys," he said, waving at the other guards. They all smiled at him and waved.

"Stop him!" I shouted before he could leave. "He stole a painting!"

The guards turned and looked at me. They all looked really confused. I could feel my face turning red.

"What are you talking about, kid?" one of the other guards said.

"He stole that Morland painting," I said, standing firm.

"What?" another guard said. "No way. The Morland painting is still hanging in the gallery."

"That's a copy," Egg said.

"Ask him what's in that black case," I said. "That will prove it."

Tom laughed. "This?" he said. "This is my pool cue." He turned to the other guards. "You guys know how much I love to shoot pool!" he said.

The other guards nodded. "Tom shoots pool a few times a week," one of them said. "I've seen his cue case lots of times."

Tom shook his head. Once again, he started for the door.

Just then, the weird man in the overcoat stepped up and took Tom's arm. "Just a moment please," the weird guy said. "I think maybe we should have a look in that case."

"Hey!" Tom replied. "Who do you think you are?"

The weird guy pulled a leather case from his coat pocket. He flipped it open to reveal a gold badge. "I'm Detective Jones, River City Police Department," he said. "Open the case."

"I knew that guy was involved somehow," Sam whispered.

"I won't!" Tom said. "I know my rights."

The detective nodded. "Very well," he said. "Let's all go take a closer look at the painting on the wall, then."

Tom swallowed. "O-okay," he said.

The detective led us and Tom back to the exhibit. He found Ms. Stanwyck and asked her to step past the velvet rope.

"Have a close look, Ms. Stanwyck," the detective said.

"At the wheelbarrow!" Egg added.

Ms. Stanwyck looked at the detective and Egg. "Okay," she said. She pulled a magnifying glass from her pocket.

"That explains why she didn't spot it earlier," Sam whispered. "Her vision isn't good enough."

"They're right!" Ms. Stanwyck suddenly exclaimed. "These strokes are definitely not Morland's! This copy isn't even as good as the one I made years ago."

The detective glared at Tom the security guard. "Ready to open that case now?" Detective Jones asked.

Tom unzipped the top of the case and pulled out a pool cue. "See?" he said. "Just a pool cue!"

"Just a pool cue, huh?" I said.

Then I suddenly snatched at the case. I reached in and pulled out a rolled-up canvas.

"What's this?" I said. I unrolled the canvas, showing the real "The Inside of a Stable."

The detective smiled at us. "Nice job, kids," he said.

"He figured it out," Sam said, pointing at me.

"What's your name, kid?" Detective Jones asked.

"Shoo," I replied. "James Shoo."

"You're a real detective, James Shoo," Detective Jones said, patting my shoulder.

"You could say," Sam added with a chuckle, "he's a real gumshoe."

Cat, Egg, and I all looked at her.

"Get it?" Sam said. "Gumshoe?"

We all shook our heads.

Sam sighed. "It's old-movie slang for detective," she said. "And James's name is Shoo?!"

I rolled my eyes and we all made fun of Sam, but really I liked the nickname.

So it stuck, and that's why I'm called Gum Shoo.

literary news

MYSTERIOUS WRITER REVEALED!

▶ SAINT PAUL, MN

Steve Brezenoff lives in St. Paul, Minnesota, with his wife, Beth, their son, Sam, and their small, smelly dog, Harry. Besides writing books, he enjoys playing video games, riding his bicycle, and helping middle-school students work on their writing skills. Steve's ideas almost always come to him in his dreams, so he does his best writing in his pajamas.

arts & entertainment

CALIFORNIA ARTIST IS KEY TO SOLVING MYSTERY – POLICE SAY

Early on, C. B. Canga's parents discovered that a piece of paper and some crayons worked wonders in taming the restless dragon. There was no turning back. In 2002 he received his BFA in Illustration from the Academy of Arts University in San Francisco. He works at the Academy of Arts as a drawing instructor. He lives in California with his wife, Robyn, and his three kids.

A Detective's Dictionary

confiscate (KON-fiss-kayt)–take away from someone

crook (KROOK)–someone who has committed a crime

evidence (EV-uh-duhnss)–something that could help solve a crime

goon (GOON)–someone hired to protect something

gumshoe (GUHM-shoo)–a detective

hoodlums (HOOD-lumz)–people who are up to no good

phony (FOH-nee)–fake

skulking (SKUHL-king)–sneaking around

suspect (SUH-spekt)–someone who may have committed a crime

telephoto (tell-uh-FOH-toh)–a special lens that helps a camera take a picture of something far away

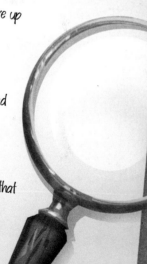

James Shoo

Ms. Stanwyk's Art Class

May 12

(A)

Famous Stolen Paintings

The strangest thing that happened on our field trip to the art museum was that a painting was stolen. Luckily, my friends and I helped catch the crook. I don't think that anyone should steal paintings.

This was not the first time a painting was stolen. One of the first recorded art thefts was in 1473. Pirates stole the painting, "The Last Judgment" by Hans Memling.

In 1911 the "Mona Lisa," a very famous painting by Leonardo DaVinci, was stolen from the Louvre Museum in Paris. It turned out that a person who worked at the museum had stolen the painting. That's what happened to the painting at our museum, to

The painting "Jacob de Gheyn III" by Rembrandt is the most-stolen painting of all time. It has been stolen at least four times from the Dulwich Picture Gallery in London. Because it has been stolen so many times, it is nicknamed the "Takeaway Rembrandt."

Even though paintings have been stolen throughout history, it is still shocking when it happens. Thieves shouldn't take paintings. Paintings should be in museums for everyone to enjoy.

Very good, James! (And great job catching the crook, too—I'm very proud.) Did you know that the Mona Lisa doesn't have any eyelashes or eyebrows? —Ms. S.

FURTHER INVESTIGATIONS

1. In this book, Ms. Stanwyk took our art class on a field trip to the art museum. Where have you gone on a field trip? If you could go anywhere on a field trip, where would you go?

2. Why did the security guard steal the painting?

3. Egg, Cat, Sam, and I made a list of suspects when we were trying to solve the mystery. Think of a mystery that needs to be solved at your school or home. Working as a group, make a list of suspects. Then solve the mystery!

IN YOUR OWN DETECTIVE'S NOTEBOOK . . .

1. The mystery in this book was solved by me and my best friends. Write about your best friend. What is she or he like?

2. Egg, Cat, Sam, and I all have nicknames. In this book, you find out how I got my nickname. Do you have a nickname? How did you get your nickname? If you could choose any nickname, what would it be, and why? Write about it.

3. This book is a mystery story. Write your own mystery story!

THEY SOLVE CRIMES, CATCH CROOKS, CRACK CODES . . . AND RIDE THE BUS BACK TO SCHOOL AFTERWARD.

Meet Egg, Gum, Sam, and Cat.
Four sixth-grade detectives and best
friends. Wherever field trips take them,
mysteries aren't far behind . . .

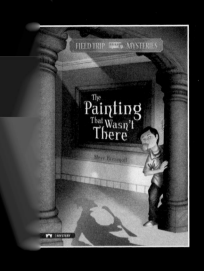

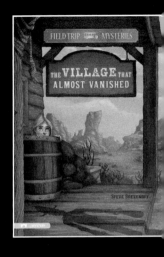

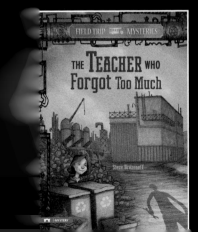

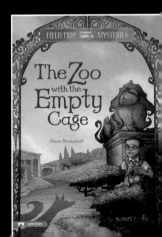

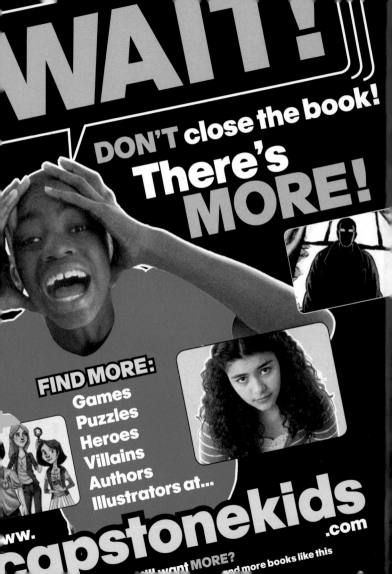